# The Pup Squad

Becky wasn't listening. She was staring down at Max, who was sniffing the air, every muscle tensed. "Max, what is it?"

The German shepherd was standing perfectly still, staring at the large brick building that was the Eagles' clubhouse.

"Max — what are you doing?" Liam began impatiently.

But Becky interrupted him. "Shh! He can hear something! Listen!"

Then both of them heard a faint *thud* inside the building. . . .

# Titles in Jenny Dale's POLICE PUP series

# THE **PUP SQUAD**

Jenny Dale

Illustrated by Mick Reid

A
**LITTLE APPLE**
PAPERBACK

SCHOLASTIC INC.

New York  Toronto  London  Auckland  Sydney
Mexico City  New Delhi  Hong Kong  Buenos Aires

ISBN 0-439-32263-4

All rights reserved. Published by Scholastic Inc., 555 Broadway, New York, NY 10012, by arrangement with Macmillan Children's Books, a division of Macmillan Publishers Ltd.

SCHOLASTIC and associated logos are trademarks and/or registered trademarks of Scholastic Inc.

12 11 10 9 8 7 6 5 4 3 2 1          1 2 3 4 5 6/0

Printed in the U.S.A.                    40

First Scholastic printing, October 2001

*Special thanks to Narinder Dhami.*

*Many thanks also to
Steve Dean and Peter Whitehead
of the Metropolitan Police Service for their
valuable advice.*

*In memory of Metpol Ashley —
whose sons and daughters,
grandsons and granddaughters
are now proudly following in his footsteps.*

# Chapter One

"GOAL!" Liam Wilson punched the air in triumph, pulled his T-shirt over his head, and ran around the yard pretending to be an airplane. Max, the Wilsons' German shepherd dog, raced after him, his bushy tail wagging wildly.

"You'd better look where you're going," Liam's twin sister, Becky, remarked as she retrieved the ball from a nearby flower bed. "Or you'll end up in the pond!"

"Great goal, wasn't it, Max?" Liam

ruffled the thick fur on Max's neck, his fingers sinking into the dog's dense brown-black coat. "Maybe I'll play for England when I grow up!"

"In your dreams!" Becky scoffed as she carried the ball back to their make-shift goalposts, two overturned flower-pots. "Come on, it's your turn to be goalie."

"Just one more shot!" Liam pleaded.

Becky grinned and kicked the ball down the lawn toward him.

Max immediately chased after it, pink tongue hanging out, and playfully attempted to nose it away from Liam.

"Max!" Liam yelled, but he couldn't help laughing.

"Maybe Max will end up playing for England instead of you!" Becky joked.

"It's great having so much space to

play soccer, isn't it?" said Liam as he gazed around the large backyard. In the distance, the hills of the Peak District stretched away as far as the eye could see. "Our old yard wasn't half as big as this."

Liam and Becky had only been living at Lark Cottage, in the Derbyshire town of Ellandale, for the last month or so. They'd moved there with their parents because their father, who was a policeman, had a new job at the Ellandale Police Station.

Officer John Wilson was not just an ordinary policeman. He was a dog handler. And Max was no ordinary German shepherd, either. He had been given to Officer Wilson as a puppy to be trained to fight crime, and he'd recently started his new job alongside his handler. But in the year that Max had been living with the Wilsons, he'd also become a much-loved member of the family.

"I wouldn't go back to live in the city for a million dollars!" Liam announced as he positioned the ball carefully on the grass. "I *love* living in Ellandale!" He took a few steps backward, then stopped to look at his twin. "By the way, Becky, have you heard anything about a soccer game being played in Ellandale soon?"

"What soccer game?" Becky asked, trying not to smile. Max was very slyly nudging the ball away from the spot where Liam had placed it.

"I heard some kids at school talking about it," Liam went on. "The Ellandale Eagles soccer team is going to play some big game."

"We can ask Julie," Becky suggested.

Julie Gibbs, who lived next door, was the first friend they'd made in Ellandale.

"Yep, good idea." Liam nodded. He swung his leg back, kicked at a ball that was no longer there, and nearly fell over.

Meanwhile, Max was sitting with the ball a short distance away, looking very pleased with himself, thumping his tail.

"Max!" Liam groaned.

"Nice one, Max!" someone called from the other side of the fence.

Julie Gibbs was standing in the yard next door. She waved, and Max bounded over, put his front paws up on the fence, and stood there on his hind legs so that Julie could pet him.

"Hi, Max!" Smiling, Julie ruffled his fur. "Aren't you a smart boy!"

"Come over and play a game with us!" Liam called.

"I can't." Julie sighed. "We're just about to go shopping." She was interrupted by the sound of frantic yapping, and she frowned. "Scooter, be quiet!"

Liam and Becky grinned at each other. Julie's Jack Russell terrier, Scooter, was a real handful.

The yapping got louder. Julie bent down, picked Scooter up, and held him over the fence so that he and Max could sniff at each other.

"You'll have to come to the Ellandale Eagles and Turnham Tigers soccer game next week," Julie said, struggling to stop Scooter from scrambling over to Max. "It's a big event in town — everyone goes to it."

"That must be the game I heard the kids at school talking about," Liam said eagerly to Becky.

"Turnham's the next town over, isn't it?" Becky asked Julie.

Julie nodded. "You probably haven't noticed yet because you haven't been here that long, but Ellandale and Turnham are always trying to beat each other at *everything*!"

Liam looked interested. "What do you mean?"

"Well, like the Christmas trees in the park every year. We always try to have the biggest. And the soccer game, of course." Julie grinned at them. "The two towns have been playing each other once a year for the past fifty years."

"Fifty years!" Liam's eyes opened wide. "Is there a trophy or something?"

"Oh, yes — and we've won it for the past nine years!" Julie told him proudly. "The game is being played here in Ellandale this time, and if we win for the tenth time, we get to keep the trophy forever!"

"Oh, we'll win!" Liam said confidently. "The Tigers don't stand a chance!"

Becky couldn't help smiling to herself. Typical Liam! He'd only been in Ellandale for five minutes, and he was already an enthusiastic supporter of the local team!

"Julie?"

At that moment, Daniel, Julie's brother, came out the back door. He had the same fair hair as his younger sister and was tall and athletic-looking. "Mom's waiting."

"Okay." Julie glanced at Liam and Becky. "I didn't tell you that Daniel's an Ellandale Eagle, did I? He's their star player!"

"I wouldn't say that, Julie!" Daniel grinned at Liam and Becky. "I hope you two are going to come and cheer for us."

"Of course we will!" Liam promised fervently. "And we'll make an Ellandale Eagles ribbon for you to wear, Max!"

Max had picked up on Liam's excitement. He bounded over to Liam, tail wagging enthusiastically, and butted him gently with his head.

"This game sounds like fun!" Becky said eagerly.

"What do you mean — fun?" Liam exclaimed, looking shocked. "This is serious stuff! Isn't it, Max?"

Max cocked his head to one side, stared up at Liam with his intelligent dark eyes, and barked in agreement.

# Chapter Two

"Wow! That's a huge trophy!" Liam said admiringly. It was a few days later, and he was standing with his nose pressed against a large glass cabinet in the town hall. It was the trophy that the two teams would be competing for the following week.

Julie's mom, Mrs. Gibbs, was caretaker at the town hall and had let Julie, Liam, and Becky come in to have a quick look at the trophy after school.

"Looks like the Turnham Tigers have

won it quite a few times, too." Becky pointed at the list of winners engraved on the front of the large silver trophy.

"But not for the past nine years!" Liam said. He turned to Julie. "What happens when the Eagles win next week and keep the trophy forever?"

"*If* they win," Becky said with a grin, but Liam ignored her.

"The Turnham Tigers have to pay for a

new trophy," Julie replied. "And then it starts all over again next year!"

"All right, you three, off you go," said Mrs. Gibbs, coming into the hall with a large bunch of keys in her hand. "I need to put out some chairs for the Neighborhood Watch meeting this evening."

"Do you want us to help?" Becky asked politely.

Julie's mom shook her head. "No, thanks, dear, it'll only take me five minutes. Anyway, didn't you leave Max outside?"

"Yes, come on, Becky," Liam said hastily, "the Eagles must have started practicing by now."

On their way to the town hall, they'd passed the Ellandale Eagles' field, and the players had been getting ready to practice.

Max was sitting patiently outside, exactly where Liam and Becky had left him. His tail started to wag as soon as he caught sight of them, but he didn't move from the spot until Liam called him over.

"I wish Scooter was like that!" Julie sighed, giving Max a pat. "He'd be digging his way into someone's backyard in two minutes!"

"Come on, Max." Liam took hold of the leash. "We'll go and watch the practice, then we'll take you for a walk."

Officer Wilson and Max worked shifts at the Ellandale Police Station, and today they'd finished work just after lunch. Liam and Becky loved it when they got back from school and Max was already home.

Max trotted obediently along as Liam, Becky, and Julie made their way over to the playing field on the edge of the town. The Eagles, including Daniel, were hard at work, sprinting up and down and doing push-ups.

Liam nudged Julie. "Daniel looks pretty fit, doesn't he?"

Julie nodded proudly. "Did I tell you he scored the winning goal in the game last year?"

"Cool!" said Liam, impressed.

"Max, what's the matter?" Becky asked as the German shepherd suddenly gave a tug at the leash and began to get excited. Then she laughed. "Look, Liam, there's Dad. Max spotted him first, as usual!"

Officer Wilson, in a blue warm-up

suit, was out for a jog and was running down the road alongside the soccer field.

"Your dad looks pretty fit, too," Julie remarked with a smile.

"Dad has to be fit to keep up with Max!" Liam grinned, giving one of Max's alert ears a gentle, affectionate tug.

Becky nodded. "He used to play soccer, too, for a team in our old town," she told Julie.

Officer Wilson spotted them and jogged over. "Hello," he said with a smile.

"Dad, you will remember that we're coming to watch the game next week, won't you?" Liam asked anxiously.

"Eight!" Becky said immediately, and she and Julie burst out laughing.

"What?" asked Liam, puzzled.

"That's the eighth time you've asked!" Becky grinned. "I've been counting!"

Liam stuck his tongue out at her. "Well, I don't want to miss it, that's all!"

"Of course we won't miss it," Officer Wilson assured Liam as he patted Max's back. "Saturday's my day off, so I'll definitely be able to come." He wiped his forehead and did a few quick stretches. "I'd better finish my run. Don't be too late getting home."

As Max watched Officer Wilson jogging off into the distance, Liam and Becky turned their attention back to the team.

The Eagles had divided into teams and started to play a short game. Liam, Becky, and Julie stood watching. Max sat patiently beside them, his head moving from side to side as he, too, kept his eye on the speeding ball.

Then Becky glanced at her watch and nudged Liam. "We'd better go," she said. "We've still got to take Max for a walk, and it's already six o'clock."

"Okay," Liam said reluctantly.

"There's going to be a big party if we win the game next week," Julie remarked as they walked with Max. "With fireworks and everything."

"What if the Eagles lose?" Becky asked, ignoring Liam's snort of disgust at the question.

"We'll have the party anyway!" Julie grinned. "We'll need cheering up!"

"It's the Turnham Tigers who are going to need cheering up!" Liam said as they walked down the winding street.

"There's someone coming," Becky said suddenly.

Julie frowned and looked up and down the empty street. "I can't see anyone," she began. Then she stopped in amazement as a boy and a girl came around the curve of the street and into sight. "How did you know they were there?"

"I didn't — Max did!" Becky laughed. "I noticed his ears perk up!"

Max was staring at the boy and girl with interest, keenly monitoring their every movement as they got closer. Both of them were tall and skinny, with red hair.

"I know them," Julie said in a whisper. "It's Robin and Sarah Barnett. They're a bit older than we are. Their big brother, Tom, is playing in the game next week."

"Is he a good player?" Liam asked.

"I hope not," Julie retorted with a grin. "He plays for the Tigers!"

"You mean they're from *Turnham*?" Liam said, dismayed. "Oh, no!"

Robin and Sarah Barnett heard what Liam said and stared at him. Robin didn't seem too bothered, but Sarah scowled.

"Hi, you two!" Julie said quickly. "Where are you going?"

"Hi, Julie," Robin replied. "We're going to Anderson's on an errand for our mom." Anderson's was a store in Ellandale that did all sorts of repairs.

"Are you looking forward to the game?" Julie went on.

"You bet!" said Robin eagerly. "We're going to win, too!"

"We'll see about that!" Julie grinned. "These are my friends Liam and Becky Wilson and their dog, Max."

"Is this the new police dog who was in the local paper a few days ago?" Robin asked, squatting down to make friends with the German shepherd.

Becky nodded. "Yes, he found a boy who was missing."

"That's pretty cool," Robin said admiringly, ruffling Max's dense brown-black fur.

Sarah was still staring at Liam. "Are *you* going to the game next week?" she asked.

"Of course we are," Liam replied.

"Bring tissues, then," Sarah retorted. "Because you'll be crying your eyes out by the end of it!"

"Very funny!" Liam snorted. "It's the Turnham Tigers who are going to be crying their eyes out — like they've done for the past nine years!"

Sarah blushed. "The past nine years don't count!"

"Oh, yes, they do," Liam shot back

quickly. "Because when we win this time, we keep the trophy forever!"

"In your dreams!" Sarah was getting quite annoyed now.

"Come on, Sarah!" Looking embarrassed, Robin grabbed his sister's arm. "See you at the game."

"Honestly, Liam, what's the matter with you?" Becky sighed as the Barnetts went off. "You two are acting like a couple of babies!"

"That Sarah Barnett made me mad!" Liam grumbled. Then he grinned. "I can't *wait* to see her face when the Eagles win next Saturday."

# Chapter Three

"What do you think, Becky?" Liam held up the banner he'd made. It read

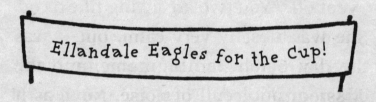

Ellandale Eagles for the Cup!

and was decorated in red and white, the team's colors.

"Excellent!" Becky said, then showed Liam her red-and-white ribbon. "And this will look great on Max's collar!"

"Class!" Liam and Becky's teacher, Ms. Kendall, sounded rather irritated.

She was usually very calm, but it was the day before the big game, and the classroom was full of noise. Now, as it got closer to dismissal, the excitement was tremendous. "Time to clean up!"

Becky quickly put the finishing touches on her ribbon as Liam and Julie cleared their table.

As soon as the bell rang, there was a stampede toward the door.

"See you at the game tomorrow, Ms. Kendall!" Liam called as he, Becky, and Julie joined the rush to leave. "You *are* coming, aren't you?"

"I wouldn't miss it for anything!" Ms. Kendall said with a smile. "Although I'd rather be playing than watching!"

There was a real party atmosphere in town as Liam, Becky, and Julie walked home. It seemed as if everyone they knew wanted to stop to talk about the game tomorrow. Lots of people had hung banners and ribbons in the windows of their houses, and there were also banners in most of the local stores.

When Liam and Becky finally got home, Officer Wilson, who had already finished work for the day, was mowing the lawn. As usual, Max had realized that Liam and Becky were close by and was waiting by the back door to greet them.

"Look what I've made for you, Max!" Becky showed him the ribbon, and Max sniffed it cautiously.

"I don't suppose you two got much work done at school today," their father remarked with a twinkle in his eye. "I expect you were discussing soccer all the time. Everyone at the station certainly was! And by the way, you're in for a surprise tomorrow when you see who the referee is!"

"Who is it?" Liam asked eagerly, but their father shook his head.

"Wait and see!" he teased.

Becky gave Liam a nudge. "Come on,

let's take Max for a walk, and we can see if anything's happening on the soccer field," she said.

Max sat up at the word "walk," and now, with a sign from Becky, he trotted into the kitchen to get his leash.

"Don't be too long," Officer Wilson called after them as they let themselves out the back door with Max. "Mom will be back home in an hour or so, and I'm cooking dinner tonight." The twins' mom, Tina Wilson, worked as a nurse in Ellandale and the surrounding towns. When Officer Wilson worked the early shift, he arrived home first and cooked dinner.

Liam and Becky nodded and then set off in the direction of the soccer field.

"It's too early for the team to start practicing," Liam remarked as they neared the field. "Most of the players will still be at work."

"No, look — there's someone there," Becky replied, squinting in the late afternoon sun.

A balding middle-aged man was pacing along the field, staring intently at the grass. Liam groaned as he realized who it was. "Oh, no, it's Sergeant Thornton!"

Sergeant Jim Thornton was one of the few people in Ellandale the twins hadn't really gotten along with so far. He sat at the front desk at the police station and was, according to Officer Wilson, very efficient.

But Sergeant Thornton was also very set in his ways, and he hadn't been enthusiastic about Max's arrival at the station. He'd changed his mind a little, though, when Max had solved the case of a missing boy within a few days of starting work!

"Hello, Sergeant Thornton," Becky called politely.

The sergeant looked up and gave them a nod. "Good afternoon."

Max wagged his tail, recognizing the policeman, but Sergeant Thornton pretended not to notice.

"How's Inky, Sergeant Thornton?" Liam asked with a mischievous grin.

The sergeant blushed.

Inky was Sergeant Thornton's big black cat. Liam and Becky had overheard him talking to Inky one day, in a rather sappy voice. It seemed that Jim Thornton had a real soft spot for his cat, even if he didn't like Max much.

"Very well, thank you," Sergeant Thornton muttered. "Now, if you'll excuse me."

Becky began to lead Max away.

But Liam stayed put. "What are you doing?" he asked nosily.

Becky grinned. Liam never could take a hint!

"I'm examining the field before the game takes place tomorrow," Sergeant Thornton said importantly.

"Why?" Liam asked, puzzled.

But Becky was quicker. "You mean, *you're* refereeing the match?"

*"What?"* Liam gasped in such a dismayed voice that Becky kicked his ankle. *"Ow!"*

"Yes, I am," Sergeant Thornton snapped, looking rather annoyed.

"Oh, great!" Liam suddenly cheered up. "You can make sure the Eagles win!"

"I'll do no such thing," Sergeant Thornton said frostily. "I will be firm but fair!"

"Oh, sure!" Liam winked at him, and the sergeant turned purple. "Is there practice tonight?"

"No," the sergeant snapped. "It's their day off, so you might as well go home." Then he stomped off down the field.

"Now you've upset him!" Becky remarked.

"Oh, I was only teasing him!" Liam grinned as they walked across the field toward the locker room. "I bet he'll be a pretty good ref, actually!"

Becky wasn't listening. She was staring down at Max, who was sniffing the air, every muscle tensed. "Max, what is it?"

The German shepherd was standing perfectly still, staring at the large brick building that was the Eagles' clubhouse.

"Max — what are you doing?" Liam began impatiently.

But Becky interrupted him. "Shhh! He can hear something! Listen!"

Then both of them heard a faint *thud* inside the building.

Max strained to get up the steps to the door, clearly wanting to find out what was going on.

"There's someone in there!" Liam gasped. "Sergeant Thornton said the team wasn't practicing today — so who is it?"

# Chapter Four

"Liam, it could be anyone!" Becky pointed out as her brother tiptoed up the steps with Max.

"Like who?" Liam muttered, trying the door. It was locked. He peered through the nearest window but couldn't see a thing because it was so dirty.

"It could be someone getting the uniforms ready for tomorrow," Becky suggested. "It could be someone making the refreshments. It could be —"

"Someone trying to sabotage the Eagles' chances of winning the trophy!" Liam interrupted urgently.

Max had sniffed the bottom of the door thoroughly but now seemed to have lost interest in it. Instead he was trying to pull Liam back down the steps.

"Stop it, Max!" Liam said crossly. "You're the one who dragged us over here in the first place!"

Becky stared at Max. "I think he wants us to follow him." She was interrupted by the sound of another, louder *thud* that sounded like it was coming from the back of the building.

"Did you hear that?" Liam gasped. "Come on!" He raced around the corner of the building, Max running alongside him and Becky in hot pursuit.

As they reached the back of the building they were just in time to see four figures running as fast as they could across the grass to the nearby gate. One of them had very familiar long red hair.

"That's Sarah Barnett!" Liam yelled. "What's *she* doing here?"

"I don't know." Becky pointed to a window that was open. "But I think she broke in!"

"What!" Liam said indignantly. He dropped Max's leash and grabbed hold of the windowsill, hauling himself up.

Becky did the same.

They were looking into the Ellandale Eagles' locker room. The uniforms had already been laid out for the game. None of the clothes had been disturbed, but Liam and Becky could hardly believe their eyes.

The whole locker room was covered with banners and ribbons in the blue-

and-white colors of the Turnham Tigers soccer team. The banners read

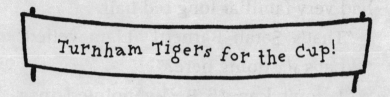

Turnham Tigers for the Cup!

and

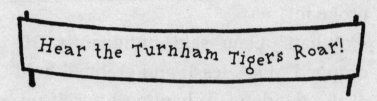

Hear the Turnham Tigers Roar!

"Look what they've done!" Liam gasped, outraged. "Quick, is Sergeant Thornton still on the field?"

They ran out to look for the sergeant, but there was no sign of him.

"I wonder which way he went?" said Becky anxiously.

"Who knows?" Liam replied. "But we know where Dad is — come on!"

* * *

"Well, there seems to have been no damage done," Officer Wilson concluded a few minutes later. "Of course, they shouldn't have gone into the locker room at all, but I gather that particular window has been broken for some time."

He looked at Liam and Becky. "It seems to have just been a joke. I don't think they meant any harm."

"Some joke!" Liam muttered. "They were trying to get us rattled before tomorrow!"

Liam, Becky, and Max had dashed straight home to get Officer Wilson, and he had immediately contacted Mr. Randall, the Eagles' manager, to come and check for damage.

The locker room had been cleaned up and the broken window fixed, but nobody wanted to make a big fuss about finding the culprits because they didn't want to spoil the big game tomorrow.

"Did you say you recognized one of the kids who did it?" Tina Wilson asked as she put chili into bowls. She had taken over cooking dinner. Max was in the kitchen, having his own dinner.

"Yes, it was Sarah Barnett," Liam said

firmly. "And I think she knew it was me and Becky, too!"

But Officer Wilson shook his head. "I thought you said you only saw them from behind."

"I did," Liam admitted. "But I recognized her red hair!"

"Well, that wouldn't stand up in a court of law!" his father teased him gently. "Don't worry about it. It was just a silly prank, and it's all been taken care of now."

"I don't trust that Sarah Barnett," Liam said as they went to Julie's house after dinner. "She's up to something!"

"Like what?" Becky asked, ringing the doorbell.

"I don't know." Liam shrugged.

"Maybe she'll try to ruin the Eagles' chances of winning the game tomorrow!"

"Oh, get real! What could she do?" Becky scoffed as Julie opened the door.

"Well, don't say I didn't warn you!" Liam muttered.

"Oh, hi," said Julie. "Come in. I'm just looking for Scooter. He's missing, and that usually means trouble!"

Liam opened his mouth to launch into the story of what Sarah Barnett had been up to when Julie suddenly turned and ran into the living room.

"I *thought* I heard something!" she said triumphantly, peering behind the sofa. "Scooter, come out, you naughty boy!"

"We'll help you," Becky offered as Julie tried to move the sofa on her own.

"He's chewing something," Julie said

as they inched the sofa away from the wall. "I don't know what it is."

Liam looked behind the sofa as it moved a little more. "It's a soccer cleat!"

"Oh, not Daniel's lucky soccer cleats!" Julie groaned. "He'll go ballistic!"

"I thought all the equipment was kept at the clubhouse," Becky said, remembering everything neatly laid out in the locker room.

"Not Daniel's cleats!" Julie explained breathlessly. "He *always* keeps them with him — he never lets them out of his sight!"

At that moment a voice floated down from upstairs. "Mom! Have you seen my soccer cleats?"

"Uh-oh!" Julie gave the sofa one last heave, and Scooter was revealed, chewing happily on Daniel's shoelaces. "Scooter, you bad boy!"

"There's only one cleat here," Liam pointed out. "Where's the other one?"

"Mom!" They could hear Daniel hurrying down the stairs, sounding distinctly worried by now. "Mom, have you seen my soccer cleats — AARGH!"

There was a loud *thump*, followed by several *thuds*.

Julie, Liam, and Becky glanced at one another in alarm and dashed out into the hall, almost colliding with Mrs. Gibbs, who'd run in from the kitchen.

Daniel was sitting on the hall carpet, white-faced and clutching his leg. A soccer cleat lay on the floor next to him. "Ow!" he groaned. "My ankle!"

# Chapter Five

"Daniel!" Julie cried. "What on earth happened?"

"One of my soccer cleats was lying on the stairs, and I tripped over it." Daniel was grimacing with pain as he spoke. "I don't know how it got there!"

Julie glanced at Liam and Becky and then at Scooter, who had trotted out into the hall to see what all the excitement was about. The little dog's ears went down, and he looked rather sheepish.

Daniel groaned. "I might have known

Scooter was behind it!" he muttered as his mom knelt down beside him.

"Does that hurt, dear?" Mrs. Gibbs asked as she gently examined his ankle.

"No, it's not too bad," Daniel said bravely. But then he winced as his mother pressed down a little harder. *"OW!"*

"I'll go and get Mom," Becky said. "She'll know what to do."

"Thanks, sweetie," replied Mrs. Gibbs, sounding worried.

"Does this mean you won't be able to play in the game tomorrow?" Liam asked, dismayed.

Daniel nodded. He looked very upset. "Mom, I'd better call Mr. Randall right away," he said.

"Let's get this ankle of yours taken

care of first," Mrs. Gibbs said firmly, helping Daniel to stand up and hop into the living room.

"But I've got to let Mr. Randall know," said Daniel. "He'll have to find another forward before tomorrow!"

"What, you mean the Eagles don't have another forward who can take your place?" Liam asked, horrified. Things were going from bad to worse.

"Well, we do, but he's not in shape to play," Daniel explained glumly as he sank into a chair. "He was going to be a sub tomorrow, but he won't last the whole ninety minutes."

Tina Wilson declared that Daniel's ankle was sprained. While she bandaged it up, Daniel called Mr. Randall to give him the bad news.

Liam groaned and sat down on the sofa, his head in his hands. "What are the Eagles going to do without their star forward?" he muttered. "We'll never win now!"

"I've got an idea," Becky said slowly.

Liam looked at her. He could usually trust Becky to come up with something useful in a tricky situation, but what on earth could she suggest this time?

Becky grinned at her brother. "What about Dad?"

"You'll be great, Dad!" Liam said encouragingly. "I bet you'll score lots of goals!"

"If I can keep going for ninety minutes, I'll be happy!" Officer Wilson grinned as he picked up his jacket. "See you at the game!"

It was the morning of the big game. After Becky's bright idea, things had moved fast. Mr. Randall had been thrilled to hear that Officer Wilson used to play soccer for his local team and that he still kept himself in shape. He insisted on going to Lark Cottage to speak to him right away, and half an hour later, Liam and Becky's father was a member of the Ellandale Eagles team.

"That was an excellent idea of yours, Becky!" Liam said happily, waving to their father. The team manager had asked him to come a few hours before the game to discuss tactics. "Dad's going to be just as good as Daniel!"

"I hope so  or nobody in Ellandale will speak to us again!" Tina Wilson joked.

"Dad will be the best!" Liam said confidently. "Won't he, Max?"

Max, who was sprawled out on the carpet, thumped his tail several times, looking up at Liam with his dark eyes.

Both Liam and Becky were nervous — especially Liam. Now, fifteen minutes before kickoff, they had arrived at the crowded field with their mom and Max, who was proudly wearing his Ellandale Eagles ribbon.

Everyone in the town seemed to have heard that Officer Wilson was taking Daniel's place on the team.

"I'm sure Officer Wilson will do a wonderful job!" called Mrs. Saunders, who ran the local post office.

"Liam! Becky! Over here!"

Julie was waving at them from the other side of the field. The Gibbs family had left about ten minutes before the Wilsons in order to get spots on the side-lines.

Daniel, who was on crutches but had a chair to sit on, could see everything from there. "I wouldn't have missed the game for anything!" he said as the Wilsons and Max came over to join them.

"Where's Scooter?" Becky asked.

"We left him at home," Julie replied.

"I don't want him running on the field and tripping someone else!"

"Unless it's a Turnham Tigers player!" Liam joked.

Becky nudged him. "There's Ms. Kendall," she said.

"There's Janie." Liam pointed out Officer Blake, their father's young red-haired colleague, who was walking around the edge of the large crowd. "She's in uniform, so she must be on duty."

Becky didn't answer. She'd just spotted Sarah and Robin Barnett arriving at the entrance. She hoped Liam didn't see them. He was likely to speak up about the events of the previous night.

Liam glanced at his watch and frowned. "I thought it was supposed to start at two o'clock, and the teams aren't even out yet."

"Don't panic!" His mom smiled. "I'm sure there's a good reason." She waved across the field at an elderly woman who had her leg bandaged. "I'm just going to go over and have a word with Mrs. Barnes. She shouldn't really be out with that bad leg of hers, but she said wild horses wouldn't keep her away!"

Even though it was only a minute after two, the crowd was beginning to get restless. Then Sergeant Thornton, looking rather sharp in his black-and-white referee's uniform, hurried out of the locker room. He looked irritated. Ignoring questions from the crowd, he beckoned urgently to Officer Blake. Her face grew anxious as he spoke to her.

Liam and Becky could see that there was a problem, but what was it?

A buzz of excitement ran through the crowd as Sergeant Thornton walked onto the field and waited for silence. "Ladies and gentlemen!" he said, his booming voice carrying to all corners of the crowd. "I'm afraid the start of the game will be delayed. I'm sorry to tell you that the trophy has disappeared!"

# Chapter Six

"What?" Liam was horrified. "The trophy's been stolen?"

Everyone in the crowd, Eagles and Tigers fans alike, was shocked. There was a lot of groaning and muttering.

"The cup was in the clubhouse until a few minutes ago, and then it vanished," Sergeant Thornton went on. "Naturally, we are doing all we can to find it."

"What a mean thing to do!" Julie said indignantly as Sergeant Thornton went off to talk to Officer Blake again. "The thief must know how much everyone's looking forward to the game."

"Maybe it wasn't a thief," Liam said.

"What do you mean?" Daniel Gibbs asked, but Becky knew exactly what Liam was going to say.

"Maybe it's someone who wants to stop the Eagles from winning the cup and keeping it!" Liam replied.

"Sabotage, you mean?" Daniel looked startled. "But that doesn't make sense. What if the Tigers win? They won't have the trophy, either!"

Liam wasn't listening. He had just spotted a familiar head of long red hair on the opposite side of the field. "Sarah Barnett!" he whispered, giving Becky a nudge that nearly knocked her over. "I bet she's got something to do with this!"

"I don't think so, Liam." Becky grabbed her brother's arm, just in case he decided to charge over there. "I saw her arrive a few minutes ago. She wouldn't have had time to take the trophy."

"You don't know that for sure," Liam grumbled, but he stayed where he was. He kept shooting suspicious glances at Sarah.

After another five minutes, Sergeant Thornton came back to talk to the crowd. Everyone fell silent immediately.

"I'm sorry to tell you that the trophy hasn't been found yet," Sergeant Thornton announced. "But we've decided that the game will go ahead. Meanwhile, the police will continue to search."

There was a subdued cheer from the crowd. At least they were going to see

the game, and maybe the trophy would
be found before it was over.

"Becky, I think we should go and look
for the trophy!" Liam said in a determined voice. "We can't let Sarah Barnett
get away with it! Max can help us."

Max looked up as he heard his name.
He stared anxiously from Liam to Becky,
picking up the urgency in their voices.

Becky thought about Liam's idea. Max was trained to pick up the scent of humans and their property. He could find something as small as a coin or an earring hidden in tall grass. But to do that, the conditions had to be right. And with so many people around, it was pretty unlikely that Max could pick out just one scent from all the others.

But Becky could tell that her brother wanted to do something. "Well, all right," she agreed. "I guess it can't hurt."

Soon the two teams came running out onto the field and began to warm up.

Liam groaned. "We'll miss the start of the game — but this is more important. Come on!"

They slipped quietly away. Their mom was still across the field, chatting with her elderly patient, and the Gibbses were too busy cheering on the Eagles to notice.

Officer Janie Blake was pacing around the clubhouse, staring intently for clues. Liam, Becky, and Max rushed over.

"Janie, I mean Officer Blake!" Liam said breathlessly. "Can we help you look for the trophy?"

Officer Blake hesitated. "This is official police business," she said sternly. "So you shouldn't be getting involved."

Liam's face fell. "We thought Max might be able to help," he muttered.

Janie couldn't help smiling. "Well, if you and Max want to have a look, it's up to you!" she said. "I don't know anything about it, though — and don't breathe a word to Sergeant Thornton!"

They followed her into the clubhouse

and into the office. The wooden base on which the trophy had stood was still on the desk. Liam went over to look at it, and Max followed, putting his paws up on the desk and sniffing it curiously.

Just then a whistle sounded outside, and there was a cheer from the crowd.

"The game's started!" Liam said grimly. "So we've got less than ninety minutes to get the trophy back! Come on, Max, let's start looking."

# Chapter Seven

"Clean as a whistle!" Liam said gloomily as they led Max out of the clubhouse. "There's no way the trophy is in there!"

"And Max would have found the thief if he'd been hiding anywhere," Becky added.

"Never mind," Officer Blake said. "You go back and watch the game."

"It'll be halftime in twenty minutes," Becky said. "We can have another look then."

Liam, Becky, and Max went back to watch the rest of the first half. The game was so exciting that the Gibbs family had hardly noticed their absence. And luckily, their mom was still on the other side of the field with Mrs. Barnes, who seemed to be a chatterbox.

The teams were very evenly matched, and each side had come close to scoring several times. But when halftime came, there was still no score.

As soon as Sergeant Thornton blew the whistle, there was a rush for the snack truck parked at the edge of the field. Julie and her mom went to buy drinks for everyone.

Becky turned to Liam. "Whoa!" she gasped. "This is too exciting for me!"

"But even if the Eagles win, we won't have the trophy!" Liam muttered. "I think it's about time Sarah Barnett confessed!" He took off before Becky could stop him.

"Oh, no!" Becky groaned. She hurried after Liam, taking Max with her, hoping she was in time to stop her twin from doing something stupid.

Liam was *sure* that Sarah Barnett had something to do with the trophy disappearing. He looked around, trying to spot her long red hair.

Everyone was taking the opportunity to stretch their legs during the break, and it wasn't easy to spot one person in the large crowd. But after a little while, Liam saw her. Sarah was standing talking to a group of kids her age.

Probably the same gang who broke into the changing room last night! Liam thought angrily. "Hey, Sarah!" he called.

Sarah Barnett turned almost as red as her hair when she saw Liam. "What do you want?" she asked nervously.

"I know it was you and your buddies who got into the Eagles' locker room last night and put all that Tigers stuff up!" Liam challenged her.

Sarah turned even redder. "I don't know what you're talking about!" she said.

"Oh, yes, you do!" Liam insisted. "And I bet you've taken the trophy, too, haven't you?" he accused. "Where is it?"

"The trophy?" Sarah repeated, looking shocked.

Just then, Becky and Max finally caught up with Liam. The second half was about to start, and everyone was hurrying back to their places.

"Of course I didn't take the trophy!" Sarah protested. "Okay, we did do all that stuff in the locker room for a laugh, but I *didn't* take the trophy!"

Liam stared at Sarah, surprised. She sounded like she was telling the truth.

"Come on, Liam!" Becky grabbed his arm and pulled him away. "Sarah said she didn't take the trophy, and I believe her."

"So do I, I suppose," Liam replied sheepishly as they walked away. "But if Sarah didn't take the cup, who did?"

When the game restarted, things went badly for the Ellandale Eagles. Five minutes into the second half, the Eagles' captain, their best defender, accidentally hit heads with one of the Tigers' forwards and had to leave the field. A substitute defender was sent in, but the loss of their captain hit the Eagles hard.

Officer Wilson and the other forward were both playing very well, but they were receiving the ball much less. The Tigers were running rings around the ragged Eagles defense.

"Look, they're all over the place!" Liam muttered as the Eagles chased back in disarray to fend off yet another attack. "Even Dad's back, defending his own half!"

Fifteen minutes later, the inevitable happened. The Tigers took a corner kick, and a big forward with bright red hair ran past the Eagles defense and kicked the ball into the net. The Tigers fans went wild.

"Oh, no! They've scored!" Liam

groaned unhappily. "I bet that was Sarah Barnett's brother, too!" Max licked Liam's hand sympathetically.

"And we only have twenty-five minutes left to catch up," Becky said quietly.

# Chapter Eight

"Oh, no!" Liam covered his eyes once again as the Tigers ran down toward the Eagles' goal. "I can't watch this!"

But this time Tom Barnett's shot just missed and grazed the top of the goal.

"Let's go see if Janie has had any luck finding the trophy," Becky said as the Tigers' fans applauded their team's latest effort. "She might have found a clue by now, and Max might be able to help."

"There's not much point in doing that,

is there?" Liam asked gloomily. "The Eagles don't look like they're going to tie the score, and the Tigers are going to score again any minute."

"Well, we shouldn't let the thief get away, whoever wins the match," Becky said.

"Okay," Liam agreed. He didn't really want to watch the game, not with the Eagles getting clobbered. He turned to his mom, who'd finally managed to get away from the talkative Mrs. Barnes. "Mom, we're just going to see if Officer Blake's found the trophy yet."

Their mom frowned. "All right," she agreed, "but don't get in the way — and come right back."

Once they were on the outskirts of the crowd, Liam, Becky, and Max went over to the clubhouse and looked around for Officer Blake. But she was nowhere to be seen.

"Maybe we could walk around for a bit and see if Max can pick up the trail," Liam suggested.

Becky didn't think there was much they could do, but she could see that Liam was too wound up to stand and watch the game, so she agreed. They wandered aimlessly over to the edge of the field, away from the crowd, following wherever Max led them.

"Oh, well, at least Turnham won't get the trophy, either, if they win!" Liam said, trying to look on the bright side.

But Becky didn't answer. Her gaze was fixed on Max, who had suddenly started sniffing the air intently, turning his head this way and that.

"What is it, Max?" Becky asked urgently.

She and Liam both glanced around but couldn't see anything out of the ordinary.

Then Liam clutched Becky's arm. "Look!"

Everyone in the crowd was intent on watching the game except for Max, Liam, Becky — and one other person. A man with a sports bag was walking quickly away from the field toward the town. As he reached the exit, he looked back over his shoulder as if he expected someone to come after him.

Max gave a short, sharp bark and began to pull Becky in the same direction.

"Is that the thief, Max?" she gasped. "Liam, what if the trophy is in that bag? Janie needs to know about this!"

"Yes, but by the time we've found her, the man will have disappeared!" Liam replied urgently. The man was now half running, half walking down the street and was already almost out of view.

Becky nodded. "You're right. Let's go, Max!" she said.

Eagerly, Max led Becky and Liam

down the street, which ran into the road that led onto Main Street.

When they reached Main Street, most of the stores were closed, and there was no one around. To their dismay, the suspicious man with the sports bag had vanished.

"Find him, Max!" Liam ordered. He and Becky both knew that a police dog's strongest weapon is its sense of smell. Their father had explained to them that when human beings are scared, their bodies give off a different scent. This scent was what police dogs like Max could use to track down criminals as well as missing people. Liam was hoping that if the man were the thief, he would be feeling very nervous, and Max would be able to sense that.

Max went down the street, seeming to

know exactly where he was going. He stopped by the pizza place for a second but wasn't distracted by the smells wafting out. He turned into the alley that ran alongside it.

Liam peered down the alley and then pulled Max sharply back around the corner. "He's there, Becky!" he said urgently. "Down by the garbage cans!"

Becky peered around the corner of the pizza place, too, as Liam gave Max a signal to sit down quietly. The man had no idea that they were there. He was intent on pulling the heavy lid off one of the large garbage cans that stood at the end of the alley.

"What's he doing?" Liam whispered as the man placed the lid carefully on the ground so it didn't make a noise. Once or twice he glanced up the alley, and Liam and Becky had to jump back out of sight.

When they risked a quick look around the corner again, the man was dragging a black plastic bag out of the bin. He untied it and pulled out the silver trophy.

# Chapter Nine

"He *is* the thief!" Liam hissed.

"Shh!" Becky said, alarmed, as the man quickly unzipped his bag and shoved the trophy inside. "We'd better run and find Janie, or he's going to get away!"

"I'll stay here with Max and stop him!" Liam began determinedly, but Becky shook her head.

"No, he might be dangerous," she insisted. "Come on, even if he runs off before we get back here with Janie, Max will be able to find him again!"

"Okay." Liam agreed reluctantly, and the three of them raced back down Main Street.

As they pounded up the lane toward the soccer field, Becky panted. "Funny, I've got the feeling I've seen the thief before."

"Me, too," Liam agreed between gasps for air. "But I don't know where."

They were almost back at the game now, and they could hear the shouts of the crowd.

"I wonder what the score is," Liam said as he pushed the gate open.

"Let's hope the Eagles have pulled ahead," Becky replied, following him and Max onto the field.

As she turned to close the gate behind them, Becky happened to glance back down the street. "Liam!" she hissed. "Look! He's coming back!"

"What?" Liam could hardly believe his ears. He stared down the street, and sure enough, the thief was hurrying back, carrying his bulging sports bag.

Liam was furious. "He must be a Tigers fan!" he gasped. "I bet he just didn't want the Eagles to get the trophy, so he hid it — and now that the Tigers look like they're going to win, he's going to put it back!"

"We've got to find Janie before he gets rid of it!" Becky said urgently.

The first place they looked was the clubhouse, but Officer Blake was still nowhere to be seen.

Liam was about to charge off to look among the crowd when Becky stopped him. "I've got an idea," she said. "Give me Max's leash."

Liam gave it to her. Becky led Max into the clubhouse and left him just behind the door.

"Sit, Max!" she said.

Max's ears immediately perked up, and he sat obediently.

"Good idea, Becky!" Liam exclaimed as Becky came out and closed the door.

They knew that Max would bark as soon as anyone approached the building — and that would hopefully be enough to keep the thief outside!

Leaving Max on guard, Liam and Becky ran off to search the crowd for Officer Blake.

While they were looking, Liam spotted their teacher, Ms. Kendall. "What's the score?" he asked, hoping that the Tigers hadn't scored any more goals.

"Oh, hello, Liam." Ms. Kendall smiled at him. "It's still one-nothing. But we're coming alive, and your dad's playing really well!"

Liam watched, his heart thumping, as his father received a pass from one of the Eagles' defenders and then made a determined run for the goal. He was stopped by a foul that won the Eagles a free kick.

"Ms. Kendall, have you seen Officer Blake anywhere?" Liam asked, checking his watch. As far as he could tell, there were only five minutes left to play in the game, plus injury time. It looked like the Eagles really had lost now.

"She was over by the snack truck a few minutes ago," his teacher replied.

Liam and Becky ran off toward the truck. The crowd of Eagles fans groaned when the free kick didn't make the goal, and Liam's heart sank again.

"There she is!" Becky shouted as she spotted the policewoman pacing slowly around the field.

"Janie!" Liam rushed up and grabbed her arm. "We've found the thief!"

"What!" Janie's eyebrows disappeared into her auburn bangs. "Are you sure?"

"Certain!" Becky cried. "Come on, or he'll get away!"

They all ran back to the clubhouse. On the way, Liam and Becky quickly explained what had happened.

As they neared the building, they could hear Max barking from behind the door. The man with the sports bag was standing outside.

"Be quiet!" the man was saying desperately. "Come on, let me in. Good dog!"

But Max wasn't paying any attention.

The man was so intent on trying to get Max to be quiet that he didn't see Officer Blake, Liam, and Becky coming up behind him.

"May I ask what you're doing, sir?" Officer Blake asked calmly.

The man almost jumped out of his

skin. He turned around. His face was white as chalk. "Um — hello, Officer Blake," he stammered.

Janie Blake raised her eyebrows. "Roger Kitson!" she exclaimed.

"You mean, you *know* him?" Liam began.

But Becky elbowed him in the ribs to make him be quiet. They had to let Officer Blake handle this.

"I'd like to know what you've got in that bag, Mr. Kitson," Officer Blake went on, pleasantly but firmly.

"Oh, really!" Roger Kitson blustered. "It seems to me that it's none of your business!"

"It is my business when I'm looking for a missing trophy!" Officer Blake replied sternly as Liam opened the door and Max bounded out.

Roger Kitson collapsed like a burst balloon. Keeping a wary eye on Max, he handed the bag over meekly.

Officer Blake unzipped it and pulled out the silver trophy.

At the same moment there was a loud roar from the Eagles' fans. Liam and Becky glanced at each other, left Max with Officer Blake in case she needed

any help, and then rushed over to the field.

They reached the goal just in time to see Joe Peters, the other forward, kick the ball into the back of the Tigers' net.

"YES!" Liam and Becky went crazy, shouting their heads off and hanging on to each other as they jumped up and down. "We're tied!"

Everyone else in the crowd was going crazy. Even Daniel Gibbs had pulled himself up from his seat and was waving one of his crutches in the air when the players raced back to the center circle.

"Right on! Now we've got to win!" Liam yelled, with an anxious glance at his watch. The game was now into injury time. There was quite a bit extra to be added on because of the injury to the

Eagles' captain, so there was still a chance for the Eagles to score again, Liam thought hopefully. Anyway, a tie wasn't as good as winning, but it was better than losing!

Both Becky and Liam were chewing their nails when the game started again. Their hearts thumped as the Tigers began to run into Eagles territory, but the Eagles' defense intercepted the ball and kicked it upfield. The ball fell right at the feet of Officer Wilson.

"Come on, Dad! You can do it!" Liam and Becky shouted together.

The Tigers' defense was chasing back, but they were too late. Officer Wilson had only the goalie to beat, and he had moved off his line to try to block the angle.

Officer Wilson hesitated. Then, instead of trying to run round the goalie, he kicked the ball delicately over his head. The goalie had no chance of reaching it. Just under the goal, the ball fell sharply and bounced into the net.

Five seconds later, Sergeant Thornton blew the final whistle.

"We've done it!" Liam and Becky shrieked so loudly their throats hurt. "We've won!"

# Chapter Ten

Everyone in the crowd was applauding, both Eagles and Tigers fans alike. The players were shaking hands with one another, and everyone was smiling.

The Eagles hoisted Officer Wilson up onto their shoulders and carried him around the field for a victory lap. Liam and Becky watched proudly, waving at their dad as he went past.

Then a murmur of surprise went through the crowd like a wave, followed by a gigantic cheer. Officer Janie Blake was walking onto the field, carry-

ing the trophy in her arms, with Max trotting alongside her.

Liam and Becky grinned at each other as their mom and the Gibbs family stared in amazement.

"What on earth has been going on?" Tina Wilson asked.

"Max found the trophy!" Liam said with a grin.

Meanwhile, Officer Blake was talking

with Sergeant Thornton, who kept looking down at Max as if he couldn't believe his ears.

Then the sergeant raised his arms for silence. "As you can see, the trophy has been found!" he announced. This was followed by another cheer. "This means that we can present it to the Ellandale Eagles, who are now entitled to keep the trophy, having won it for the past ten years."

Liam and Becky cheered loudly along with all the other Ellandale fans as the Eagles' captain went up to claim the silver trophy.

"It only remains for me to say" — Sergeant Thornton swallowed hard as if something was stuck in his throat — "that it was Max, our local police dog, who caught the culprit, and we owe him a big thank-you."

Everyone clapped while Max sat wagging his tail, enjoying all the attention. Liam and Becky were bursting with pride. What a great day it had been for the Wilson family!

"So who *is* Roger Kitson, Janie?" Liam asked. "Is he a Turnham Tigers fan?"

Janie shook her head. "No, actually he lives in Ellandale!"

The postgame party was in full swing in the town park. The Turnham team and their fans had also been invited. There was a DJ, and snack trucks provided refreshments.

Officer Blake glanced at Officer Wilson. "Is it okay to tell them?"

The twins' father laughed. "Well, everyone else in town knows the story!"

"What story?" Liam asked curiously.

"Roger Kitson's brother Jim used to be on the Eagles team," Officer Blake explained. "He was cut at the beginning of the season for stealing from club funds, and I guess Roger thought he'd get some revenge. He tried to return the trophy as soon as he thought the Eagles were going to lose."

"But when did he take the trophy — and put it in the garbage can?" Becky wanted to know.

"Well, he took it just before the start of the game," Janie replied. "Then he went off to hide it after Sergeant Thornton announced that it was missing. Everyone was so shocked, no one noticed Roger Kitson leaving the field with his sports bag!"

"What's going to happen to him now?" Becky asked.

"Well, I arrested him and took him back to the station," Officer Blake went on. "It's up to the Eagles whether they want to charge him or not."

"Oh, well, at least it didn't spoil the game!" Becky put her arm around her father's neck. "You were great, Dad!"

"Yes, you're our hero!" Tina Wilson smiled. "And so is Max!"

Max immediately got to his feet and looked for someone to pet him.

"Good boy!" Becky kissed the top of his head. "Where are you going, Liam?"

"Just something I've got to do," Liam said vaguely as he took off across the park.

Curious, Becky followed him, and Max, who was never far away from the twins if he could help it, went, too.

Liam made his way over to Sarah

Barnett, who was sitting on the grass chatting with her brother Robin and drinking lemonade.

"Um — sorry," Liam muttered. "I shouldn't have accused you of taking the trophy like that."

Sarah turned pink. "That's okay," she mumbled. "I shouldn't have gone into the locker room. It was a stupid idea."

"I'm glad we've got that straightened out!" Robin said with a grin. He reached over to pet Max. "Well done, Max — you saved the day! How did he find the thief, anyway?"

"Max could have smelled the trophy in the bag," Liam said. "Or he might just have realized that the man was up to something!" He quickly explained how dogs can pick up human scents — and how humans give off a different scent when they're frightened. Sarah and Robin listened, fascinated.

"You should come to Turnham sometime," Sarah said, giving Liam and Becky a can of lemonade each. "We could get a soccer game going between some of the kids from Turnham and you and your Ellandale pals."

"Great idea!" Liam said, his face lighting up. "We'd win, of course, just like we did today!"

"No, you wouldn't!" Sarah retorted.

"Yes, we would!" Liam stopped as Max nudged his leg gently but insistently.

"Max wants you to stop arguing!" Becky remarked.

Liam grinned. "We'd better do what

Max wants," he said. "He's the hero of the day — along with Dad, of course!"

"To Max, the hero!" Becky said, raising her can of lemonade for a toast.

"To Max, the hero!" the others echoed, doing the same.

Max gave a long, loud woof that seemed to say, "All in a day's work for a police pup like me!"